HELLO, I'M THEA!

I'm *Geronimo Stilton*'s sister. As I'm sure you know from my brother's bestselling novels, I'm a special correspondent for *The Rodent's Gazette*, Mouse Island's most famous newspaper. Unlike my 'fraidy mouse brother, I absolutely adore traveling, having adventures, and meeting rodents from all around the world!

The adventure I want to tell you about begins at Mouseford Academy, the school I went to when I was a young mouseling. I had such a great experience there as a student that I came back to teach a journalism class.

When I returned as a grown mouse, I met five really special students: Colette, Nicky, Pamela, Paulina, and Violet. You could hardly imagine five more different mouselings, but they became great friends right away. And they liked me so much that they decided to name their group after me: the Thea Sisters! I was so touched by that, I decided to write about their adventures. So turn the page to read a fabumouse adventure about the

THEA SISTERS!

nicky

Nicky

COLETTE

Name: Colette

Nickname: It's Colette, please. (She can't stand nicknames.)

Home: France

Secret ambition: Colette is very particular about her appearance. She wants to be a fashion writer.

Loves: The color pink.

Strengths: She's energetic and full of great ideas.

Weaknesses: She's always late!

Secret: To relax, there's nothing Colette likes more than a manicure and pedicure.

Colette

VIOLET

Name: Violet

Nickname: Vi

Home: China

Secret ambition: Wants to become a great violinist.

Loves: Books! She is a real intellectual, just like my brother, Geronimo.

Strengths: She's detail-oriented and always open to new things.

Weaknesses: She is a bit sensitive and can't stand being teased. And if she doesn't get enough sleep, she can be a real grouch!

Secret: She likes to unwind by listening to classical music and drinking green tea.

Violet

Name: Paulina
Nickname: Polly
Home: Peru
Secret ambition: Wants to be a scientist.
Loves: Traveling and meeting people from all over the world. She is also very close to her sister, Maria.
Strengths: Loves helping other rodents.
Weaknesses: She's shy and can be a bit clumsy.
Secret: She is a computer genius!

PAULINA

PAULINA

Name: Pamela

Nickname: Pam

Home: Tanzania

Secret ambition: Wants to become a sports journalist or a car mechanic.

Loves: Pizza, pizza, and more pizza! She'd eat pizza for breakfast if she could.

Strengths: She is a peacemaker. She can't stand arguments.

Weaknesses: She is very impulsive.

Secret: Give her a screwdriver and any mechanical problem will be solved!

Pamela

Geronimo Stilton

Thea Stilton
AND THE
CHERRY BLOSSOM ADVENTURE

Scholastic Inc.

New York   Toronto   London   Auckland
Sydney   Mexico City   New Delhi   Hong Kong

ISBN 978-0-545-22772-8

www.geronimostilton.com

Published by Scholastic Inc., 557 Broadway, New York, NY 10012. SCHOLASTIC and associated logos are trademarks and/or registered trademarks of Scholastic Inc.

Text by Thea Stilton
Original title *Il mistero della bambola nera*
Cover by Arianna Rea, Paolo Ferrante, and Ketty Formaggio
Illustrations by Alessandro Battan, Elisa Falcone, Claudia Forcelloni, Michela Frare, Daniela Geremia, Roberta Pierpaoli, Arianna Rea, Maurizio Roggerone, and Roberta Tedeschi
Color by Tania Boccalini, Alessandra Bracaglia, Ketty Formaggio, Elena Sanjust, and Micaela Tangorra
Graphics by Paola Cantoni

Special thanks to Beth Dunfey
Translated by Julia Heim
Interior design by Kay Petronio

20   19   18   17   16   15   14 15 16/0

Printed in the U.S.A.   40
First printing, March 2011

A SPECIAL GIFT

It was a hot midsummer day. It was gorgeous outside, but I was trapped inside my mouse hole, scampering <u>back</u> and *FORTH* like a rat in a maze. I was waiting for a very **important** package, and the mailmouse was late!

You see, I am a special correspondent for The Rodent's Gazette. I'm always traveling for work, and I'm ready to leave for a new

ADVENTURE at the drop of a cheese slice. Waiting has never been my strong suit!

After what seemed like an eternity, Mercury Whale, the mailmouse from Whale Island, finally arrived. He always

brings me news from my dear *friends*, the THEA SISTERS. A few months ago, I was invited back to my alma mater, Mouseford Academy, to teach a course in adventure journalism.

That's how I met *Colette*, *Nicky*, PAMELA, PAULINA, and **Violet** — they were my students. After we solved a mystery together, the five mouselets decided to call themselves the THEA SISTERS in honor of our friendship. I am very proud of them!

Before Mercury even had a chance to *ring* the bell, I rushed to the door and threw it

open. "Finally!" I exclaimed, **beaming**.

The poor rodent almost **JUMPED** out of his fur. He stammered, "M-Miss Thea, I came to give you this —"

"Package, yes, yes, I know!" I interrupted **impatiently**.

Mercury seemed stunned. "Uh . . . yes, but surely you don't know that it comes from —"

"From **JAPAN!**" I said, **CUTTING** him off. "And I know just what's inside...."

Japan is a country made up of many islands — some large and others very small — arranged in an arc east of the Asian continent.

Tokyo is the capital of Japan and is on the largest island of the archipelago. A good 13 million of Japan's 127 million inhabitants live there! Japan is rich with natural marvels, like forests, mountains, lakes, and volcanoes. The country is divided into eight regions, as shown on the map above.

In fact, Colette, Nicky, PAMELA, PAULINA, and **Violet** had already alerted me to the fact that a special gift would be arriving. They were all waiting for me at a big summer FESTIVAL in Japan! It'd been so long since I'd seen those five mouselets, I was more impatient than a cat with a mouse in its claws. I said a *QUICK* good-bye to Mercury, grabbed my suitcase, and scurried off to the airport.

But what was inside the package, you ask? Well, if you want to find out, you'll have to keep reading!

It all started with a special student exchange organized by **MOUSEFORD ACADEMY**. . . .

JAPAN, HERE
WE COME!

One bright spring day, a **MouseAir** plane was coming in for a landing in the faraway country of JAPAN.

Mouseford Academy had organized an EXCHANGE program with the famouse Yoshimune Academy of Kyoto. The five THEA SISTERS had immediately volunteered to join the TRAVELERS. There was nothing those five mouselings loved more than visiting new places! They had been preparing for the trip for months, and their enthusiasm was sky high.

After a few layovers, they landed at the Osaka airport. From there, they were bound for Kyoto, one of the **oldest** cities in Japan.

"These are going to be the three most

FABUMOUSE months of our lives!" exclaimed Pam.

"I've been wanting to visit Japan since I was a wee mouseling!" Nicky agreed.

Paulina **FOLLOWED** them. She had her snout deep in her TRAVEL GUIDE to Japan. "We need to start studying, mouselings!" she said **ANXIOUSLY**. "We'll be taking

KYOTO

Region: Kansai
Prefecture: Kyoto
Population: Over 1.4 million
Features: The architectural treasures of Kyoto are world famous.

Kyoto

SOME HIGHLIGHTS OF THE CITY

Nijo-jo (the Nijo Castle)
Built around 1600, this castle is a magnificent example of traditional Japanese architecture. Because of numerous fires over the years, the castle has been partially rebuilt, but you can still admire the painted sliding doors and the inlaid wood.

Kinkaku-ji (the Golden Pavilion)
Kinkaku-ji was built near the end of the fourteenth century. It is nicknamed the Golden Pavilion because its top two stories are coated in gold leaf.

Kyoto was named Japan's capital by the emperor **Kammu** in 794 AD. It remained Japan's capital city until 1868, when the capital was moved to Tokyo. It's still possible to visit the striking imperial palace, called **Kyoto Gosho**, which rises in the center of the city. The palace is surrounded by a vast park.

Kyoto has a rich history, and it's filled with perfectly preserved monuments. Today it's one of the most famous tourist destinations in Japan.

Karesansui (the rock gardens)

These splendid gardens were designed to express the ideas of harmony and peace through a precise placement of stones and moss. The stones are positioned on a stretch of sand or gravel, in which winding lines and concentric circles are traced. One of the most famous rock gardens in Japan can be found in Kyoto, at Ryoan-ji Temple.

Ohanami (cherry blossom viewing)

Ohanami is a tradition that dates from ancient times. Every year in early spring, the people of Japan gather for picnics to observe the beauty of the cherry blossoms (**sakura**).

classes like real Japanese **students**."

"Have no fear. I'll be here to help you!" **Violet** reassured her. "When I was a mouseling, I studied Japanese, and I still remember a lot."

"Thanks, Violet, or should I say ... *arigato**!" chirped Colette, bowing deeply.

Professor SPARKLE and Professor MARBLEMOUSE were the chaperones for the Mouseford

Professor Mousilda Marblemouse

Professor Batholomew Sparkle

---

* **Arigato** means *thank you* in Japanese.

group. They were very busy giving advice to all their students.

"At first, it might be **DIFFICULT** for you and the Japanese students to become friends, since you don't **squeak** the same language," **WARNED** Professor Sparkle. "But after a little time studying together, you'll learn to understand each other!"

After scrambling to claim their luggage, the group from Mouseford **left** the airport. A bus with the Yoshimune Academy logo was waiting to take them to Kyoto. The **TRiP** lasted a little more than an hour. The five mouselets had their snouts **pressed** against the windows the whole time, pointing out **SIGHTS** to one another.

At **YOSHIMUNE ACADEMY,** Professor Nishikawa, the school's director, was standing in the center of the courtyard. Behind him, all the

teachers and the **students** were lined up. It was very **exciting** for the rodents of Mouseford!

After a long moment, Professor Nishikawa approached the **MOUSEFORD** professors, bowed, and **smiled**, shaking their paws. "On behalf of all the professors and students of Yoshimune Academy, **welcome**!"

The Japanese mouselets all shouted, "WELCOME TO JAPAN!" Then the line of students broke down as everyone scurried to meet the new arrivals.

There was an **EXCHANGE** of names and greetings between the students of the two academies. When they couldn't understand each other with words, the students found other ways of **communicating**. From their pockets and pawbags, they pulled out **DIGITAL** music players, cameras, and the latest cell phones.

Director Nishikawa **winked** at his colleagues from Mouseford. "It really is true: **MOUSELINGS** are the same all over the world!"

The **bow** is a typical courteous Japanese greeting. It can convey many different things, including apology, gratitude, and respect. The longer and deeper the bow, the more respect it expresses for its recipient. For a casual hello among friends, a very slight bow is enough. But when asking for forgiveness, you must bow really deeply!

ONE OF US!

After this **warm** welcome, the moment had come to show the guests their dorm rooms.

A *gracious* mouseling in a school uniform approached the THEA SISTERS and made a **SLIGHT** bow. "*Konnichiwa**! My name is **KUMI NAKAMURA**, and I will be your guide here at the academy." She had a *sweet* and sincere smile; the THEA SISTERS immediately liked her.

"Nice to meet you, Kumi!" said Nicky, giving her paw a **vigorous** shake. "My name is Nicky, and this is Pamela, Violet —"

Before she could finish squeaking, Kumi finished the list: "And these last two must be Colette and Paulina!"

The mouselets looked at one another in

* *Konnichiwa* means *hello* in Japanese.

KUMI NAKAMURA

surprise: Had the students of Yoshimune really *memorized* the names of their guests?

Kumi explained **immediately**. "I know your names because you are the THEA SISTERS! I've been so eager to meet you in the fur!"

Seeing the perplexed expressions on the

mouselets' snouts, Kumi added, "I have followed all of your adventures, thanks to Thea Stilton's **BOOKS**: She is a writer who really knows her cheese! You mouselets have become my idols! Come on, let me show you where you'll be staying here at the *academy*."

As they walked along the academy's corridors, Kumi continued SQUEAKING cheerfully. "The mystery you solved in Paris was really **exciting**! Not to mention Australia — that mountain you climbed was **incredible**!"

Pam stopped in her tracks. She'd been taken by a sudden idea. "Chewy cheesecake with CHOCOLATE on top! Since Kumi knows us so well, why don't we make her an honorary Thea Sister?"

"**YESSSSS!**" *Colette, Nicky,*

PAMELA, PAULINA, and **Violet** agreed. They gathered around, smiling at their new friend, who looked happy and a bit overwhelmed.

SUMMER FESTIVAL!

The students from Mouseford had the remainder of the **DAY** to rest and get adjusted. Colette, nicky, PAMELA, PAULINA, and **Violet** decided to pass the time with their new friend **KUMI**.

Violet was **curious**. "You know everything about us; now tell us something about you!"

"That seems only fair," said Kumi. "Well, if you really want to get to know me . . . come with me!"

The five mouselets **FOLLOWED** Kumi through the academy's many long corridors. Finally, Kumi flung open a shiny red door.

"This is my favorite place in the entire world!" she **squeaked** with excitement.

The mouselings found themselves in a

room filled with **colorful** paintings, ribbons, fabric swatches, scissors, colored pencils, paints, other art materials of all kinds, and mannequins covered with glittering fabric.

"This is the **Art** and **Dance** Club," Kumi explained. "Here at Yoshimune, we take TRADITIONAL classes, but we also have a club that organizes shows, exhibits, and concerts. This year, I'm the president!"

The THEA SISTERS LOOKED around with their eyes open wide.

"I've studied traditional Japanese dance since I was very young," Kumi continued, "but I also know ballet and modern dance. My dream is to bring the **richness** of other cultures to Japan. I want to unite the rodents of the world through dance!"

Kumi's **EYES** shone as she squeaked.

The THEA SISTERS immediately understood that in front of them stood a very SPECIAL mouse.

Suddenly, another student burst into the room like a *whirlwind*. "Kumi! I've finally found you!" Then she noticed the others and added **coldly**, "Oh, I didn't realize you brought company."

Kumi didn't seem to notice the girl's sudden **CHANGE** of tone. Kumi introduced the THEA SISTERS to her good friend Sakura.

Sakura gave a **courteous** smile and a very slight bow. Then she turned back to Kumi as if the THEA SISTERS weren't there. "I've been looking for you forever! We need to work on the *yosakoi*, remember?"

"Of course!" exclaimed Kumi, SLAPPING her paw against her cheek. She turned to the THEA SISTERS. "I would love to show you!"

Sakura gasped. "But they can't . . ."

"Well, why not?" responded Kumi.

"Excuse me, but what is this yosi-thingy?" Colette asked.

"It's a fabumouse summer festival!" Kumi burst out enthusiastically. "Every year, hundreds of people get together to DANCE through the streets of the city of Kochi, on Shikoku Island!"

"This year, Kumi and I are in charge of the choreography and the COSTUMES," Sakura added proudly. "Our academy has participated since the very first year."

"Ooooh, can we help? PLEASE, PLEASE, PLEASE?" begged Colette.

Kumi nodded enthusiastically. "Sure!

CHOREOGRAPHY

Choreography is the art of creating and directing dance steps and movements in sequence. It comes from two ancient Greek words: **khoreia,** which means "dancing in unison," and **graphia,** which means "writing."

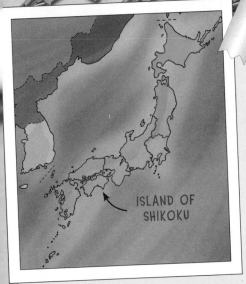

ISLAND OF SHIKOKU

YOSAKOI MATSURI

In Japan, the changing of seasons through the course of the year is an occasion for fun and colorful festivals, called **matsuri**, which take place in different regions of the country.

The **Yosakoi Matsuri** takes place on the island of Shikoku every August. It was organized for the first time in 1954. During the festival, large groups of people parade around the city, dancing the traditional **yosakoi naruko** to a tune called **"Yosakoi-bushi."** The rhythm of the music is kept by castanets called **naruko,** which farmers used in ancient times to shoo away crows from their crops.

Today, each group can create their own costumes, music, and choreography for the yosakoi. There are only three rules that must be respected:

1) Each group must have 150 people or fewer.

2) Everyone must use **naruko** clappers.

3) The **"Yosakoi-bushi"** must be used in at least part of each group's musical arrangement.

You can help make the **COSTUMES**. . . ."

"And I can help with your musical arrangement!" proposed Violet.

Nicky began to *JUMP* up and down like a kangaroo. "Hooray! I'll find someone to lend me a guitar. That way we can play a duet, Vi!"

"I know some DANCE moves that will loosen you up! I can teach you if you want," added Pam *earnestly*.

The mouselets were all in agreement: They'd go back to their rooms to freshen up from their flight. Then, that very afternoon, they would visit the city to shop for materials for the *festival*.

The only one who didn't seem enthusiastic about the way things were going was Sakura, who began to **SULK**. She found an excuse not to join the group.

Less than an hour later, Kumi **knocked** on the door of the THEA SISTERS' room. Paulina went to open it . . . and almost didn't recognize her! "But . . . but . . . Kumi, is that really you?!"

Kumi was dressed in colorful clothes instead of her school uniform. And her fur

was full of multicolored barrettes and **shiny** clips!

Colette scurried over to admire her close-up. "Wow! Kumi, you look amazing! Where did you get those boots? They are fabumouse!"

"Well, thanks," Kumi said, blushing. "The uniform is fine for school, but when we're heading off CAMPUS, we can dress as we like!"

Pam was enthusiastic. "I'm really starting to like it here! If I like the food as much as everything else, I'll have no problem giving up **Pizza** for three months!"

The mouselets grinned at each other. Their adventure in Japan was off to a super start!

A MYSTERIOUS PHONE CALL

That first afternoon went by in a FLASH, and the next few days were very busy. In the mornings, Colette, Nicky, PAMELA, PAULINA, and **Violet** took classes with their schoolmates at Yoshimune Academy. In the afternoons, they RACED OFF to help **KUMI**.

Sakura participated in the preparations for the yosakoi festival, but she seemed less enthusiastic about the THEA SISTERS than a cat on a rodent-free diet.

After two weeks of study, the *professors* decided to give

SAKURA

the students some **FREEDOM**: four days of fun with their new JAPANESE friends!

"Sakura and I have organized everything. We're going to take you on an unforgettable trip!" Kumi promised her new friends.

Their first stop was the *HOT SPRINGS* of Kurama, near Kyoto, with an overnight stay in a real Japanese *onsen ryokan*!

The mouselets agreed to meet up the next morning at the Kyoto train station.

"This **station** is like a city inside the

ONSEN RYOKAN

An **onsen** is a hot spring, or a place where water runs from the ground at a very high temperature. In Japan there are more than three thousand hot springs, and the Japanese love to visit them. The hot baths tone the body and relax the mind. Sometimes the **onsen** are connected to small inns called **ryokan**.

city!" exclaimed Paulina, looking around in **wonder**.

Escalators packed with rodents ran up and down to different levels. On every floor were shops and restaurants, and there was even a **tHeateR**!

"Hurry up! We'll miss the train!" Sakura called to Paulina and Nicky, who couldn't stop taking P I C T U R E S.

The train ride lasted only thirty minutes, but the **VIEW** from the mouselings' **WINDOW** changed as soon as they left the city. Glass and **CEMENT** were immediately replaced with majestic green **MOUNTAINS** and patches of colorful flowery shrubs.

Pam could hardly pry her snout from the window. "Now it seems like we're on another planet!" she exclaimed.

"You're right, Pam!" confirmed Kumi. "These extremes of country and city are part of Japanese **culture**. We love the **TREASURES** and traditions of our past, but we also have our eyes pointed toward the FUTURE."

Soon they arrived at KURAMA, an *enchanting* town with colorful streets. It was filled with fancy shops and tiny two-story wooden houses.

For that evening, the mouselets had reserved a room with an outdoor **POOL** at the *onsen ryokan*. After changing out of their travel things, they immersed themselves in hot water, watching the vapors rise toward the sky, which was fading into a gorgeous red **sunset**.

Surrounded by the peacefulness of the forest, the mouselings immediately relaxed. They **chatted** about everything.

Right after the bath, the mouselets had a big Japanese dinner in the hotel dining room.

"That was **whisker-licking** good,"

sighed Pamela, patting her belly.

Just then, Kumi's cell phone rang. She looked at the small screen for a moment, and a WORRIED expression crossed her snout. She excused herself and hurried from the room before answering.

Colette followed her with her eyes. "Something here smells STINKIER than old blue cheese, mouselings!"

"Of course something stinks!" Sakura snapped. "I guess Kumi hasn't filled you in."

THE PUPPET
THEATER

Sakura looked smug. She seemed pleased
to know something they didn't. "Kumi wants
to enroll in the special DANCE and theater
production school in Paris —"

"Yes, we know!" interrupted Colette, a bit
sharply.

"Kumi has great talent!" added Paulina.

Sakura nodded, then grew SERIOUS.
"But surely you don't know that her father is
a great master of the Bunraku theater. He
wants Kumi to continue the family tradition
instead of going to dance school."

"The Bunraku theater is the puppet theater,
right?" asked Violet.

BUNRAKU:

Bunraku is a type of classic theater that was developed in Japan during the Heian period (794 to 1185 AD). It's also known as **ningyo joruri**: **Ningyo** means "doll" or "marionette," and **joruri** is a story that is sung with accompaniment by a three-stringed instrument called a **shamisen**.

Every Bunraku troupe is composed of puppeteers, a shamisen player, and a narrator, or chanter (**tayu**). The marionettes are about two-thirds the size of a person and are made with great care.

BUNRAKU MARIONETTES

1. Head
2. Shoulders
3. Arms
4. Torso
5. Ring of bamboo that forms the hips
6. Ropes
7. Legs

THE JAPANESE MARIONETTE THEATER

OMOZUKAI

HIDARIZUKAI

TAYU

ASHIZUKAI

SHAMISEN player

The main puppeteer, called **omozukai**, moves the head and the right arm of the marionette. The first assistant, or the **hidarizukai**, moves the left arm, while the second assistant, the **ashizukai**, moves the legs or the long costumes of the characters. The omozukai is the only one who can show his face; the assistants must wear hoods. The most important role is that of the narrator, known as the **tayu**, who sings with the notes of the **shamisen player** and tells the story. The tayu must be able to create the atmosphere of the drama with his or her voice and must make each character and his or her emotions unique.

"You mean like puppets . . . for **young mouselings**?!" asked Pam in surprise.

Sakura smiled scornfully. "You don't understand. Bunraku is an ancient art, the only one like it in the world!"

"The Bunraku marionettes are special," explained Violet. "They are very large, and three rodents **maneuver** each puppet."

"Well, we know that Kumi deeply respects tradition," Nicky replied. "But her dreams are important, too!"

Sakura's eyes flashed with **ANGER**. "Do you think I don't know that?! We've tried to reason with her father a **THOUSAND** times, but he has decided that Kumi should become an *omozukai*, like him. Surely you don't think *you* five mice will be able to change his mind!"

With that, she turned and **STOMPED** out of the room.

There was a long pause. Then Pam burst out, "She sure has her whiskers in a *twist*!"

The other mouselings all laughed. Pam always knew how to break the TENSION. But soon the mood grew serious again.

"Maybe we won't be able to change her father's MIND, but we must do everything we can to SUPPORT Kumi!" Violet declared.

"That's right, Vi!" agreed Nicky. "That's what friends are for."

ON THE SHINKANSEN!

The next day, the mouselets left bright and early. Their destination: TOKYO!

They were going to travel on the famous Shinkansen superexpress **train**. The sleek and *superfast modern* train would take them to TOKYO — almost 250 miles away — in only two hours and twenty minutes!

SHINKANSEN

Japan's high-speed train line is called **Shinkansen**. It is sometimes referred to as the bullet train, because the express trains on this line can reach speeds of 186 miles per hour, allowing them to connect the major cities of Japan in record time.

Some of the trains have very unusual names: NOZOMI ("hope"), HIKARI ("light"), and finally, KODAMA (a traditional name for the spirits of the woods).

Paulina read her **TRAVEL GUIDE**. "We'll be traveling on a train that runs on the Nozomi service. *Nozomi* means 'HOPE.'"

Kumi saw the puzzled expression on Pamela's snout and winked at her. "Don't worry, Pam — it's the fastest train, and it's always on time!"

Pam **grinned**. "So instead of 'hope,' maybe they should have called it 'certainty.'"

Everyone **BURST OUT** laughing. Kumi was in a good mood again, and the THEA SISTERS thought it best not to ask any questions about the previous night.

The train left right on time, and soon Kyoto was far behind them.

"Look, it's **Mount Fuji**!" exclaimed Kumi, pointing out the window.

The THEA SISTERS turned. Before their eyes appeared an *enchanting* sight: the

mountain **stretching** toward the sky. Its sides reached gently up to its slightly flattened top, which was covered with SNOW. The mouselings were AWESTRUCK by the incredible sight . . .

. . . AND THEY WERE JUST AT THE BEGINNING OF THEIR FABUMOUSE JAPANESE ADVENTURE!

A TOKYO FOR EVERYONE!

Tokyo left the mouselets **breathless**: Everything was RICH with light and COLORS that they'd never imagined!

"Welcome to the city where anything is POSSIBLE!" exclaimed Kumi.

Sakura pointed out the subway entrance to the THEA SISTERS. "Well, there's lots and lots to **see**, so you should really get going."

"Are you kidding, Sakura?! *We* will be their guides!" declared Kumi, ignoring Sakura's **disappointed** expression.

Colette had very clear ideas about what she wanted to see. "I read somewhere that there's a HUGE neighborhood with all the latest Fashions!"

"That's right, the **famouse** Shibuya neighborhood," confirmed Kumi. "You're going to **love** it, Colette!"

"My book says there's also an entire area dedicated to new **TECHNOLOGY**!" added Paulina.

"Uh-huh, that's Akihabara, where we'll find all the latest gadgets!" Kumi **smiled** with satisfaction: She knew each of the mouselings' favorite things to do! For Violet, she'd planned a tour of **MUSEUMS** and the charming **historic** district of Asakusa. For Pamela, she thought of the **colors** and the rhythm of the Harajuku district. And finally, for Nicky, there was the **natural** beauty of Ueno Park!

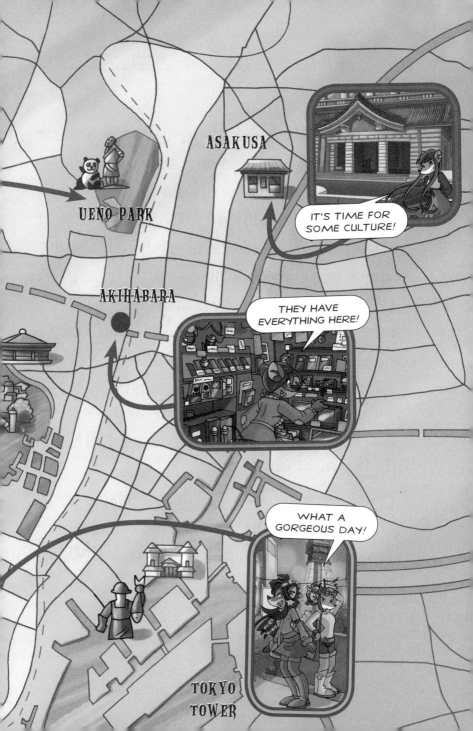

Over the next two days, the THEA SISTERS threw themselves into an exhausting but exciting tour. They didn't want to miss even the tiniest corner of that FABUMOUSE city!

Sakura followed them grudgingly. She complained constantly about the HEAT, the crowds, and how much her paws **ached** from all the scurrying about. In short, she was the only one not having fun!

By the afterNOON of the second day, the mouselings had explored most of the city from top to bottom. That was when KUMI brought them to a very special place.

"This is one of the most popular hangouts for YOUNG MICE like us!" she explained, pointing to the entrance of a BUILDING covered in neon lights.

"But, Kumi, this is *our* karaoke shop!" protested Sakura.

"Karaoke Shop?!" said Pam. "So it's a store for . . . karaoke?"

"More or less," said Kumi with an air of mystery. "You'll see: It will be really fun! Come on, follow me."

Kumi scampered into the shop, said hello to the mouse behind the counter, and headed **straight** toward a side door.

The THEA SISTERS followed her curiously.

KARAOKE

Karaoke is a favorite pastime in Japan. All you need is a well-known song, a microphone, a screen for the lyrics, and your voice! Inside a karaoke shop, you can find rooms equipped with the most modern lighting and music systems. You can stay there for hours, singing with your friends. You can even order lunch or dinner.

A moment later, they found themselves in a room without windows. It was furnished with couches, tables, and a **HUGE** screen on the wall.

KUMI made sure all her friends were comfortable. Then she flipped a switch. Suddenly, the room was filled with *FLASHING* neon colors. The screen **lit up**, and music started to **BLAST** through hidden loudsqueakers.

Pam picked up a microphone.

"All right, mouselings . . . time to get in touch with our inner divas! Let's squeak our hearts out!!!"

A NEW FRIEND

Sakura had a sullen **pout** on her snout. She didn't want to sing, and she even began YAWNING! It wasn't that she was tired; she was just **JEALOUS** of the attention Kumi was paying the THEA SISTERS.

So after a while, Sakura decided to go back to the hotel. But as soon as she was outside the karaoke shop, she got an **IDEA**. She took out her cell phone and sent a quick **text message**.

Kumi is in Tokyo! she typed, and left the address of the karaoke shop. Then she scampered away, more satisfied than a cat who had swallowed a canary.

When the mouselings **LEFT** the shop an hour later, someone was waiting for them

outside: a tall blond rodent with a **gentle** air. As soon as he spotted Kumi, he waved.

Colette saw him first. "Hey, Kumi, there's a mouse over there who seems to know you."

"That's **Holger**, a dear friend of mine from **SWEDEN**!" Kumi exclaimed.

Holger approached the group of mouselings. He looked a bit awkward.

"Hey there, **Holger**!" Kumi said *cheerfully*. "Have you come to sing karaoke, too?"

The blond mouse shook his snout. "I'm here for you, Kumi. Didn't you know?"

KUMI'S expression changed. "But how did you know where to find me?" Then she realized the **THEA SISTERS** were watching, and she hurriedly introduced the new arrival. "**Holger** is a real Bunraku theater **ARTIST**, and for many years he has been my father's most faithful assistant."

Holger shook paws with the mouselings a bit **STiFFLY**. Then he turned back to Kumi. "Your father heard you're in Tokyo. He would like to invite you and your **friends** to an evening dedicated to true Japanese **TRADITIONS**."

You see, it was Kumi's father that Sakura had **texted**!

Violet could tell at once that the invitation made Kumi feel **uncomfortable**. So she quickly piped up, "We will be happy to come with you, Kumi!"

"It will give you an opportunity to show your friends the *cherry blossoms*," Holger added, bowing to the THEA SISTERS. "If you haven't seen them already, that is . . ."

"The cherry blossoms!" Paulina squeaked excitedly, pulling out her **TRAVEL GUIDE**. "Yes! I've been longing to see them, and I think that's the only thing we haven't crossed off our to-do list!"

Kumi HESITATED for a moment, but when she looked around at the mouselings, they were all smiling and nodding. She was convinced. "Okay, let's go!"

A STRANGE MOUSE

After a short subway trip, the mouselings and **Holger** reached Kumi's family's home. The neighborhood was inside a beautiful park. All the houses were made of WOOD, built in a traditional style, and surrounded by luxurious gardens. But the **streets** didn't have any names: If Holger and Kumi hadn't been there, the THEA SISTERS would never have found the Nakamuras' house!

"Here in TOKYO, only a few streets have names," explained Kumi, smiling.

Nicky was *SHOCKED*. "It must be hard to be a mailmouse around here!"

As they headed down the lane to Kumi's house, they noticed a tall mouse with a serious air standing out front. He was wearing a *kimono** and talking to a very **SKINNY** rat dressed in a business suit.

"The one in the KIMONO is my father," said Kumi.

The conversation between the two rodents seemed very **ANIMATED**, so the little group

MR. NAKAMURA

MR. ISHIKURO

* A *kimono* is a type of traditional Japanese clothing.

waited before approaching Kumi's father.

The rodent in the suit seemed annoyed. "Be reasonable. . . . You know that the show needs funds this year," they heard him say.

Kumi's father shook his snout, looking serious. "I know you are squeaking in good faith, but without the princess there can be no show!"

"But I *insist*! Please accept my offer; it's more than generous." All at once the rodent in the suit noticed the mouselings and Holger, and he fell silent.

The THEA SISTERS exchanged perplexed looks: It seemed as though their arrival had interrupted a very important and very PRIVATE conversation!

"Mr. Nakamura, Mr. Ishikuro, may I introduce Colette, Nicky, PAMELA, PAULINA, and **Violet**," said Holger politely.

Mr. Nakamura greeted the mouselings with a deep bow, but the expression on his snout was **SERIOUS**.

Mr. Ishikuro gave a very shallow bow. Then he turned to leave. "Well, Kumi, maybe you will be able to reason with your father!" he said. "He is **STUBBORN**, but we shall see who has the **LAST SLICE** of cheese!" He bowed once more and climbed into a **black limousine** parked at the end of the lane.

"He was in such a **HURRY** to leave!" Paulina **OBSERVED** under her breath.

The other mouselings had gotten the same impression. They nodded thoughtfully.

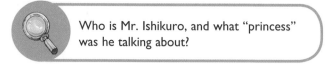

Who is Mr. Ishikuro, and what "princess" was he talking about?

THE ROOM OF WONDERS

As soon as Mr. Ishikuro had gone, Mr. Nakamura turned to Kumi and the THEA SISTERS. "Come in, and **WELCOME**! These days, Tokyo is all about everything that's new and foreign, but here you can taste the flavor of real JAPANESE traditions!"

The mouselets bowed politely. Then Kumi's father asked Holger to accompany them to a room where they would be able to freshen up and prepare for the evening.

The THEA SISTERS were a bit SURPRISED by Mr. Nakamura's welcome, which was polite, yet

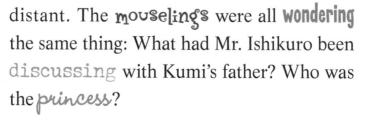
distant. The mouselings were all **wondering** the same thing: What had Mr. Ishikuro been discussing with Kumi's father? Who was the *princess*?

Kumi and Holger exchanged glances: The moment had come for explanations.

Holger gestured for the mouselets to follow him down a corridor between **SLIDING** doors. He led Kumi and the THEA SISTERS into a great room reserved for Bunraku puppets.

The mouselets could hardly believe their eyes: Along the walls were many **splendid** puppets, including warriors in **ARMOR**, fine ladies with complicated and sparkling hairdos, and **FUNNY** characters with **SCARY** faces.

The THEA SISTERS looked around in wonder. Holger smiled, pleased. "Mr.

Nakamura is a master of Bunraku," he explained. "His school is one of the most important in the country! Unfortunately, these days Bunraku attracts fewer and fewer **spectators**. We get by only thanks to donations from foundations."

"And from wealthy people who are *passionate* about Bunraku, like Mr. Ishikuro!" Kumi added.

Holger **nodded**. "These puppets are of great value, but the real Nakamura family treasure is the one we call the *princess*: a marionette that dates back to the very first Bunraku companies! Mr. Ishikuro came from his home near Kyoto just for her."

"Oooh!" exclaimed Violet, impressed.

Colette **ELBOWED** her friend, asking under her breath, "We are talking about a long, **LONG** time ago, right?"

Violet **nodded**. "That's right, Colette! The princess is about **FOUR HUNDRED** years old!"

"**AMAZING!**" commented Pam. "So, can we check out this **ANCIENT** relic? She sounds cool!"

Kumi shook her snout regretfully. "No, I'm afraid not. The princess is hidden in a **SECRET** place that only my father and I know about. She's shown to the public only once a year."

"For Kumi's **father**, the princess represents the SPIRIT of Bunraku," added **Holger** seriously. "He would *never* agree to sell her!"

The Princess

CLUE!

Paulina began to understand the strange conversation they'd overheard. "Oh, i get it. So Mr. Ishikuro would like to buy the *princess.*"

"Exactly!" Holger said. "Mr. Ishikuro is an **OLD** family friend, and he has always helped us, but **MONEY** is not enough to keep tradition alive. You also need study and **PASSION.**"

The THEA SISTERS smiled. Mr. Nakamura's Swedish apprentice seemed to love the Bunraku theater just as much as a native JAPANESE rodent!

When **Holger** noticed their looks, he

Mr. Ishikuro wants the precious princess marionette, but Kumi's father has no intention of selling her.

blushed from the tip of his snout to the tip of his tail.

KUMI came to his rescue. "Now come on, **mouselings**. We need to get ready for the **TEA** ceremony."

THE TEA CEREMONY

Holger accompanied the mouselings to another room. "You can change in here, but please be *quick* about it!"

"Change?!" replied Colette, alarmed. "But I don't have anything to wear! Not for a *ceremony*!" She was a big believer in being dressed appropriately for every occasion.

"Don't worry, Colette. My father has thought of everything!" Kumi said, reassuring her. She pawed her friend a very **soft**, light package.

Colette lifted up the paper wrapping. Inside was precious embroidered fabric. With sparkling eyes, she quickly revealed her new garment: a splendid pink *yukata**!

"**Look!** There's one for each of us!" noted Violet. "The COLORS are *perfect* for us!"

---

* A yukata is a lightweight kimono.

With Kumi's help, the mouselings tried on their outfits. They completed their new looks with hair **ornaments**, belts, white socks, and lovely traditional WOODEN sandals, which took some practice walking in.

Holger passed by to call them: He had also changed, and looked elegant in his *traditional* outfit. He led them to a small waiting room near the *garden*, where Kumi's father would meet them.

YUKATA:
lightweight kimono

KANZASHI:
hair decorations

OBI:
sash or belt

TABI:
socks

GETA:
sandals

In his dark kimono, Mr. Nakamura seemed even more **AUTHORITATIVE** and severe, but when he saw the mouselets, a **bright** smile crept onto his **snout**. "I am happy that you liked my gifts. Now, if you would **follow me** . . ."

"Oh, thank you! I **love** tea, especially with lemon . . . ," commented Colette with a giggle, but she stopped when she noticed a flash of **DISAPPROVAL** cross Mr. Nakamura's snout.

"The **TEA** ceremony is very ancient, and different from how it is in the West!" Paulina whispered. "I **read** in my guidebook that it can be pretty complicated. Let's hope we don't mess up."

"Don't **WORRY**. Just do what I do and everything will be fine!" Kumi said, **reassuring** them.

They washed their paws in a **STONE** basin along the walkway. Then they passed through a small doorway and found

THE TEA CEREMONY

The tea ceremony is one of the oldest traditions in Japanese culture. The whole ceremony lasts about four hours and involves a complex ritual, during which the invited guests eat a seven-course meal and drink two different types of **matcha tea**. Sometimes only the final part of the ceremony is performed. It lasts no more than an hour and requires only one type of tea to be prepared.

themselves in the tearoom. It was **simple** but HARMONIOUS.

Kumi's confident gestures, combined with the quiet atmosphere, had a calming effect on the THEA SISTERS, who were able to relax and appreciate the ancient ritual. As for Kumi's father, he observed the mouselets' courteous behavior with SatisFaction.

When the ceremony was **OVER**, it was already evening. "I would be very **honored** to show you the wonders of our country," Mr. Nakamura proposed.

"*Ohanami!*" exclaimed Kumi radiantly. "You **absolutely** cannot miss this, mouselings!"

Mr. Nakamura **looked** at his daughter affectionately. He gave her a sweet *smile*. "Good! Kumi, let's take our guests to discover the *yozakura!*"

"Ooh!" Violet squealed. "He means it's time for our *cherry blossom* tour," she explained to her friends.

Paulina nodded. "Japan's cherry blossoms are legendary for their beauty." She bowed to Kumi and her father. "It is our honor to have you as our guides and hosts!"

Ohanami means "to observe the blossoming of the flowers." Weather forecasts predicting the blooming of the flowers are watched carefully, since the blossoms last only a week or two.

From the end of March to the beginning of May, when the cherry and plum trees are in bloom, many people gather in parks to celebrate with a picnic. The festivities continue even into the night, when ohanami becomes the **yozakura** celebration.

The blossoming of the cherries has become a symbol of tranquility — of the peaceful internal state that comes from being in the presence of the rhythms of nature.

AN AMBUSH AMONG THE CHERRIES!

Before the little group headed toward the park, Holger said good-bye, but he promised his new friends that he would visit them at YOSHIMUNE ACADEMY.

When the THEA SISTERS, Kumi, and her father arrived at the festival, the mouselings found a breathtaking spectacle: Hundreds of rice paper lamps shone among the blooming cherry and plum trees. White petals and others as pink as powder puffs drifted through the air like snowflakes. Out among the cherry blossoms, the world seemed a truly magical place.

"It's like being inside a cherry blossom snow globe!" Paulina said breathily.

Colette nodded. "Isn't it amazing? I don't think I've ever seen any place so *beautiful*."

The air was warm, and the sweet smell of flowers surrounded the mouselings and Mr. Nakamura as they walked along a carpet of the soft fallen *petals*. The whole park was immersed in a dreamlike atmosphere. The paper lanterns spread their **glow** through the blossoms, sending GLiMMERS of light into the peaceful night.

Adding to the evening's perfection was that the tension between Kumi and her father seemed to be **disappearing**, slowly but surely.

"What a lovely evening!" sighed Violet.

"We've discovered so many **MARVELS** over these last few days, but this place is the best of all!" Paulina echoed.

Suddenly, Pam frowned. "Well, we'd better

enjoy it while it lasts, because tomorrow we have to leave TOKYO and return to the academy."

"But surely **KUMI** and her father will see each other in August for the ʊoʃakoi feʃtival!" Nicky pointed out.

Suddenly, the atmosphere completely changed. Kumi stopped smiling and shot her father an apprehensive look.

Mr. Nakamura stopped walking, and a severe expression returned to his face. "I will not be at that celebration."

"But it's a very important event for your **daughter**!" protested Paulina.

Nicky nodded. "Yes, **KUMI** is organizing an amazing *dance* this year for the academy: You simply cannot miss it!"

Kumi **sadly** shook her snout and whispered, "It's true, *Otosan**, it would make me so **HAPPY** if you would come! You could see with your own eyes that there's nothing wrong with updating traditions —"

Mr. Nakamura cut her short. "**NONSENSE**, Kumi! I will never watch the yosakoi festival: Get that into your head!"

The **THEA SISTERS** exchanged **FEARFUL** glances. And to think that just a few minutes earlier, father and daughter had been getting along so well!

It seemed like things couldn't get any worse. Then, suddenly, three suspicious rodents in dark clothes and masks appeared

* Otosan means *father* in Japanese.

CLUE!

in front of the little group! A moment later, three more scoundrels leaped from the branches of a **TREE** and **SURROUNDED** them. They closed in on Mr. Nakamura.

"**Helllllp!!!**" shouted Kumi. There were many other rodents wandering the park's

paths — surely someone would be able to help them!

But it was USELESS: In an instant, the six masked strangers had grabbed her father, GAGGED him, and scurried away with him! They were so quick that the mouselets were left standing there, PETRIFIED.

Kumi's father had just been *ratnapped*!

Six masked rodents took Kumi's father! Who could they be, and what do they want with him?

A DIFFICULT MOMENT

Kumi and the THEA SISTERS *rushed* after the **RATNAPPERS**, but they had already disappeared without a TRACE.

Grief-stricken and worried, the mouselets returned to the Nakamura house. **KUMI** was in **SHOCK**, and *Colette*, *Nicky*, PAMELA, PAULINA, and **Violet** had no intention of leaving her alone. They would do everything they could to help her!

The first thing they did was call Holger, who arrived in a flash. He was able to answer many of the amateur **detectives'** questions about who might want to harm Mr. Nakamura.

"My father doesn't have **enemies**!" Kumi kept repeating. The mouselings could tell she could hardly believe what had happened. "He is an esteemed **artist** who is respected by everyone. Who could have done such a thing?!"

The **mouselets** could only shake their snouts in sympathy and try to comfort her.

Less than an hour after the **RATNAPPING**, a black **limousine** stopped in front of the Nakamura house. Pam and Paulina exchanged glances.

"Well, would you believe that?" Pam murmured.

"It's Mr. Ishikuro," said Paulina.

The WEALTHY arts patron emerged from his luxurious car and entered the house. He seemed agitated. "I was on my way to apologize to my dear friend for my strong words earlier when I heard the incredible news. I can't **believe** it! Are there any suspects?"

Nicky GLANCED at Kumi's sad snout and declared, "Not yet, no. But we're working on it!"

Mr. Ishikuro looked ASTONISHED. But the mouselings were unfazed.

"That's right! CONFUSING cases like this one are just our cup of cheese," said Pam.

The color momentarily returned to Kumi's snout, and she smiled faintly. Colette gave her

a **big** hug while Paulina reassured her. "Have **courage**, Kumi! We'll stick by you until we've found your father!"

For a moment, hope **lit** the room's dark atmosphere.

But Violet noticed that someone didn't seem too *happy*. "Is there something wrong, Mr. Ishikuro?"

The businessman *flinched* and then quickly replied, "Uh, no, no, of course not! I just thought that it would be better if **KUMI** went back to Kyoto with you, instead of having to stay in Tokyo waiting to hear from the **RATNAPPERS**. At a time like this, she should be with her friends."

Kumi shook her snout decidedly. "Oh no! I can't **LEAVE** now. I have to wait for news of my father."

"But, my dear, there's absolutely *nothing* you can do here!" Mr. Ishikuro said with

CLUE!

conviction. "Go back to Kyoto and pull yourself **together**. I will worry about everything on this end!"

The THEA SiSTERS didn't like his tone at all: It seemed like Mr. Ishikuro was trying to get **RID** of them! But why?

At that point, Holger **came forward**. The young rodent put a paw around Kumi's shoulder and whispered sweetly, "Mr. Ishikuro is **RIGHT**, Kumi! It won't do you any good to stay here and wait by the phone. I will stay here and call you with every bit of news, I promise!"

Holger was like family to Kumi, so she let herself be convinced. Together, she and the THEA SiSTERS returned to the hotel to prepare for their **sad** journey back to Kyoto.

> Why did Mr. Ishikuro insist that the mouselets leave the Nakamura house? Hmmm . . .

A TRUSTY ASSISTANT

Over the next few days, it was very **hard** for Kumi to return to her regular life at the academy. She felt really **down**, waiting to hear news about her father, and she wasn't able to concentrate, not even at the Art and Dance Club meetings.

Sakura immediately noticed that her friend had **CHANGED** after the trip to TOKYO, but didn't know why. **KUMI** had decided she didn't want anyone else at school involved in the **UGLY** situation, so she didn't tell Sakura what had happened.

But because Kumi was so distant and distracted, Sakura thought that Kumi didn't want to be her **fRieNP** anymore. And

Sakura was sure that it was all because of the THEA SISTERS!

Meanwhile, Colette, Nicky, PAMELA, PAULINA, and **Violet** were doing all they could to comfort their friend. One day, as they were working on the costumes for the *Yosakoi*, Colette saw that **KUMI** had placed her **NEEDLE** on the table and was gazing sadly out the window.

It's all because of the Thea Sisters!

To **lift her spirits**, Colette took her friend's paw and said, "You'll see, Kumi: Everything will be all right. Holger seems like a trustworthy rodent."

Kumi's eyes *softened*. "He is! For many years he has been my father's best assistant, and he's like a member of my FAMILY."

"He seems really **PASSIONATE** about Bunraku," observed Paulina.

Kumi nodded. "He has dedicated his life to learning Bunraku! He came to JAPAN

from Sweden when he was only eighteen years old so he could **learn** from my father, and since then, he has never **LEFT**." She paused and then added, "**Holger** would be the perfect successor to my father, but our family tradition says that the *omozukai* must be JAPANESE."

"What a shame!" **SIGHED** Violet.

"Yes, my father is very stubborn about tradition—" **KUMI** stopped herself. She was silent for a while, thinking of her imprisoned father.

"Don't you worry, Kumi," Pam declared. "We're going to get your father back. I just know it!"

Nicky nodded. "You can **COUNT** on us!"

MR. ISHIKURO'S PLAN

The next morning, Kumi had a visitor: **Holger** had arrived from TOKYO. Kumi and the THEA SISTERS immediately gathered at the Art and Dance Club room, which was completely **deserted** at that hour.

Holger began telling the mouselets the news. "We've received a message from the **RATNAPPERS**: They are asking for a mountain of *yen** as ransom. They want more than even Mr. Ishikuro can gather in time for their deadline!"

Kumi was worried. "Kumi, I don't want you to get your tail in a *twist* over this," Holger said. "Mr. Ishikuro has already come up with a plan to **FREE** your father and

* The *yen* is Japan's national currency.

turn the **RATNAPPERS** over to the police!"

"We will help, too!" declared Nicky, who was always ready for ***action***, especially when it meant helping a friend.

"Thanks, but that won't be necessary," responded Holger with a smile. "The plan requires just one rodent: **KUMI**!"

Kumi's snout was tense and PALE, but her squeak was firm and filled with resolve:

"I will do whatever is **necessary**. I owe it to my father."

"There is just one thing left to do," Holger announced. "We must get the *princess*!"

Mr. Ishikuro's plan was **simple**: Instead of paying the ratnappers **MONEY**, they would give them the precious marionette.

"The princess must be worth a fortune!" cried Colette in surprise.

"It's **priceless**, but we don't have any other choice if we're going to set a **trap** for those rotten rodents!"

MR. ISHIKURO'S PLAN

WE WILL GIVE THE RATNAPPERS THE PRINCESS INSTEAD OF THE MONEY.

HOLGER WILL WAIT FOR THE RATNAPPERS AND EXCHANGE THE PRINCESS FOR MR. NAKAMURA!

Holger explained. "Once the meeting point is established, I'll wait for the **RATNAPPERS** and **EXCHANGE** the marionette for Mr. Nakamura. At the moment we make the trade, Mr. Ishikuro will arrive with the **POLICE**!"

KUMI thought it over for a minute and then agreed. "I **TRUST** you, Holger, and I will go get the *princess*, but there's just one condition: *I* will take her to the **RATNAPPERS** myself. I know my father would want it to be that way. Besides, I can't stand waiting around any longer!"

"*Right on, Kumi!*" said Pam. "We're not

AS SOON AS WE MAKE THE EXCHANGE, MR. ISHIKURO WILL ARRIVE WITH THE POLICE.

THE RATNAPPERS WILL BE ARRESTED, AND KUMI'S FATHER WILL BE FREE!

about to stay here twiddling our paws! It's time for action!"

"Uh-huh!" Paulina said **emphatically**. "We promised we would help you, and that's what we'll do!" The rest of the mouselets nodded in agreement.

Kumi's eyes grew misty with emotion. She squeezed her friends' paws tightly. "I don't know how to thank you, mouselings! You will be my warriors, just like Momotaro!"

"**HA HA HA**, it's true! We really need a dog, a monkey, and a pheasant!" agreed Holger, **BURSTING** with laughter so contagious that even Kumi had to smile.

The THEA SISTERS looked at one another in confusion.

"Dogs and monkeys?" said Violet. "What are you rodents squeaking about?!"

THE FABLE OF MOMOTARO

Holger and Kumi GIGGLED.

"It's an old **Children's** story," Holger explained. "All the JAPANESE mouselings know it, right, Kumi?"

"When I was young, I always wanted someone to read it to me," agreed Kumi, smiling. "If my father was busy, I would bring my book to Holger, and he could never say no! You see, the fable of Momotaro is about how you can overcome any problem with a little help from your friends.

JUST LISTEN..."

THE FABLE OF MOMOTARO

LONG AGO, AN OLD COUPLE LIVED IN A PEACEFUL COUNTRY HOUSE. THE COUPLE HAD NO CHILDREN, BUT THEY LIVED A QUIET AND HAPPY LIFE ON THEIR FARM. . . .

One day, the old woman went to the river to wash her clothes. There she saw a giant peach floating on the water. She decided to give it to her husband as a gift.

When the old couple split open the peach, they were shocked: inside was a beautiful baby boy!

The husband and the wife immediately decided they would raise the boy as their son.

They named him Momotaro, which means "first son of the peach." The boy grew up into a strong and intelligent young rodent.

One day, Momotaro decided to prove his worth. He left to challenge the terrible monsters on the legendary island of Onigashima.

On his journey, Momotaro met a dog, a monkey, and a pheasant. He was so generous to the three animals that they decided to help him on his mission.

Thanks to his courage and the help of his friends, Momotaro defeated the terrible inhabitants of the island and took their treasure.

The four friends returned to Momotaro's village, where the old couple greeted them joyously.

Hearing Momotaro's story, the village people elected him leader of the town. For many long years, he led with wisdom, with the friends who had stood by his side.

As soon as **KUMI** finished her tale, Pam gave a deep bow. "Let me have the honor of being your warrior monkey, Kumi!" she **joked**.

"Oh no, not a chance! I want to be your primary primate!" declared Nicky.

Violet gave a **tinkling** laugh. "Okay, in that case, I will be the pleasant pheasant!"

Paulina and Colette looked at each other. "Guess that makes us the **POWERFUL** dog!" said Paulina.

Colette shrugged. "Well, if I have to be a dog, I'm going to do it with style!"

Momotaro's company was **complete**!

THE PRINCESS'S HIDEAWAY

The next morning, the THEA SISTERS woke up early. They were going to accompany Kumi to the precious princess's **HIDING PLACE**.

As they were leaving the academy, they were so busy chattering that they didn't notice someone watching them.

It was **Sakura**. When she saw the group *scampering* along together, her jealousy surged. She was still in the dark about Mr. Nakamura's **RATNAPPING**, so she was clueless about Kumi's situation. But she was determined to get her friend back. So she decided to take action!

Meanwhile, Colette, Nicky, PAMELA, PAULINA, **Violet**, and **KUMI** were headed to the outskirts of the city. After half an hour or so, they reached a **DIRT PATH** surrounded by farms.

Kumi stopped in front of the entrance to an **old** Japanese house surrounded by lovely **cherry blossom** trees. "A poet built this house a long time ago. Welcome to Rakushisha!"

The THEA SISTERS looked around, taking everything in: the SIMPLE straw roof, the

Rakushisha is a famous traditional Japanese house. It is very simple and made of natural materials. Originally, it belonged to the poet **Mukai Kyorai**. The house's name means "the house of the fallen persimmons." According to legend, the poet woke one morning and found that the persimmons he'd grown had fallen overnight during a storm.

The house has clay walls and a straw roof. Short poems called **haiku** are inscribed on stones in its garden, and the walls are adorned with poems written in ink in Japanese characters.

ancient wood, the **smooth** stones, and the poetry written on the clay walls. It was one of the calmest, most **peaceful** places they'd ever seen!

There was no doubt: This was the perfect hideaway for a princess!

The house's guardian knew Kumi well. He had been a friend of her father's since they were in SCHOOL, and Mr. Nakamura had trusted him with his most valuable possession.

When **KUMI** told him what had happened to her father, the guardian immediately gave her a precious **EBONY** case.

At that moment, Kumi's cell phone rang. It was Holger!

The mouselets scurried back to the academy at once.

An Important Appointment

The meeting with the **RATNAPPERS** was set for eight that evening. It would be held not in Tokyo, but near the academy in Kyoto. So the THEA SISTERS and Holger agreed to gather in the Art and Dance Club room before the meeting to figure out the details of their **PLAN**.

Meanwhile, **KUMI** returned to her room to prepare. She was just about to leave when she heard someone squeak, "**Hi, Kumi!**"

Kumi was so tense she almost **JUMPED**

out of her fur. But she relaxed when she saw
Sakura standing in the doorway to her room.

"Alone at last!" her old friend said. "What
happened to your new friends? They sure
STICK close to you!"

For a moment, Kumi was tempted to fill
her in on everything that was happening. But
after one glance at her watch, she changed
her mind. She didn't have time!

"I'm sorry, Sakura, I need to go now,"
Kumi said. "I will explain everything to you
later, when things have calmed down again!"

"Oh, there's nothing to explain!" Sakura
said sulkily. "If you prefer the company of
those mice, then go find them! I certainly
won't be the one to stop you!"

Kumi was STUNNED. "What? What are you
talking about?! I don't prefer them to you!
It's just that —"

At that moment, the **bells** of the academy clock tower interrupted her, sounding the time with their deep chimes: It was **SEVEN-THIRTY**!

She turned to her bed and picked up the case with the **precious** marionette. While Kumi's tail was turned, Sakura reached over and grabbed Kumi's cell phone, then **hid it** in her uniform pocket.

KUMI was in such a hurry that she didn't

notice anything. "Sakura, please try to understand. I am terribly late for something very important! We'll squeak about this later . . . I promise!"

Sakura watched her friend RUSH OFF. She was feeling very hurt. "Oh, you think you're late for a date with your precious THEA SISTERS, Kumi," she muttered. "But what will you do when they don't SHOW UP? And they won't even be able to warn you. . . . You'll have to sit waiting for them FOR HOURS! What will you think of your

dear new friends then?"

Sakura had a trick or two up her tail! She hurried off to put her plan into action.

TRAPPED LIKE RATS IN A CAGE!

Meanwhile, the THEA SISTERS and **Holger** reviewed the **PLAN** for the zillionth time. Everything was figured out down to the very last whisker.

"We will follow Kumi from **afar** so the ratnappers don't notice us," said Violet.

"Then we'll wait for the **RATNAPPERS** to bring Mr. Nakamura for the exchange," said Paulina.

"And we'll catch them by **SURPRISE** and keep them there until the **POLICE** come!" finished Colette triumphantly.

Holger was **JUMPIER** than a mouse who'd accidentally wandered into a cat shelter. "Be careful! We just need to make

sure the **RATNAPPERS** don't get away. . . .
Don't take too many risks!"

"Don't worry, **Holger**!" Pam said,
reassuring him. "We know how to handle
slimy sewer rats like these!"

At that moment, they heard the academy
clock **STRIKE**. Nicky called them all to
order. "Let's **shake a tail**, mouselings!
Kumi is probably already on her way."

The five mouselets and Holger headed for
the door, but it was LOCKED!

They pulled, they pushed, they banged,
and they squeaked as **loudly** as they could,
but nothing worked. Someone had locked
them in! But who?!

On the other side of the door, **Sakura**
smiled in satisfaction. She was completely
unaware of the **TERRIBLE** trouble her trick
would cause!

KUMI, meanwhile, had arrived at the meeting spot: the beautiful **garden** around the Imperial Palace of Kyoto. The night was silent, and the **moonlight** illuminated the cherry trees, whose **blossoms** sparkled like crystals.

Kumi was tense and worried: She didn't see the THEA SISTERS anywhere, and the **RATNAPPERS** were about to arrive!

Apprehensively, she began searching her pockets for her CELL PHONE, but it was missing! She must have left it in her room. *Succulent sushi with* SWISS *on top!* Kumi thought. *How could I have been so careless?*

More important, how could the THEA SISTERS and **Holger** have abandoned her at such a desperate moment?!

WAY TO GO, COLETTE!

Back in the Art and Dance Club room, **Holger** and the **mouselings** were desperately dialing Kumi's CELL PHONE.

"She's not answering!" PAULINA said anxiously.

Holger shook his snout in dismay. "And neither is Mr. Ishikuro! I can't reach him. He should have been here by now, ready to have the police intervene, but he seems to have **disappeared**!"

"OH GOOD GOUDA, we can't just stay locked in here at such a time!" Pam burst out.

"Just leave everything to me, mouselings!" **Holger** said suddenly. "I'll handle it! I'll

Why isn't Mr. Ishikuro answering his phone?

knock down the door with my secret **power punches**!"

The THEA SISTERS looked at one another in surprise. At this point, they were willing to try anything to **escape** from that room!

Holger twisted himself up like a **pretzel**. He fixed his eyes on the door and then balanced on one **paw**.

Pam and Nicky could barely stifle their giggles.

Paulina nudged them. "Shhh!" she whispered. "Maybe he knows karate!"

Meanwhile, Colette was busy rummaging through her favorite pink purse. "Ooh! Here it is!" she declared at last. "Forget your power punches, Holger! We can open the door with *this*!"

Colette pulled out a PINK HAIRPIN.

Her friends stared at her in disbelief. Colette inserted the hairpin into the lock, just like rodents do in action MOVIES. After a few minutes, the pin clicked a mechanism in the door, and the door swung open!

"Way to go, Colette!" cheered Nicky, throwing her paws around her friend.

"Come on, let's move our paws!" cried Pam.

WHAT A BETRAYAL!

Meanwhile, Kumi was waiting at the meeting place. Shivering in the chilly evening breeze, she glanced around nervously, looking for the **RATNAPPERS**. While she stood alone in the dark, even the **SHADOWS** of the cherry blossoms made her whiskers quiver.

Suddenly, she heard quick PAWSTEPS approaching. . . .

TAP! TA-TAP!   TAP! TA-TAP!

Kumi trembled from her snout to her tail. Then she saw that it was the THEA SiSTERS and Holger!

The five mouselets were out of **BREATH** from their run, but they hugged their friend in relief.

"**Phew!** We . . . were . . . afraid . . . we

wouldn't . . . make it in time!" gasped Paulina.

"Running a . . . rat race . . . wasn't exactly part of our plan," huffed Colette.

"Someone tried to stop us!" explained Holger, who was also out of **BREATH**.

Their relief lasted only a moment, however, because the six **RATNAPPERS** suddenly emerged from the **SHADOWS**. But there was no sign of Mr. Nakamura!

CLUE!

Where have we seen the mouse Holger is unmasking?

"**WHAT A BETRAYAL!**" yelled Holger in alarm. "This isn't an exchange — it's a **trap**!"

"These **crooks** just want to steal the *princess*!" added Nicky as she grabbed one by the belt.

CLUE!

The **mouselings** did their best to protect Kumi and the princess, but the masked mice were well trained.

The **THEA SISTERS'** only hope was the arrival of the police Mr. Ishikuro had promised, but they never **appeared**.

"*Gotcha!*" yelled Holger suddenly. He'd grasped one of the criminals by the mask and revealed his **UGLY** snout.

But at that moment, another masked mouse managed to pull the case out of Kumi's paws.

> Mr. Ishikuro promised he would show up with the police — but where are they?!

"**NOOO!** They've got the princess!" cried Kumi, **TERRIFIED**.

By then, it was too late. Just as quickly and silently as they had arrived, the six **masked mice** slunk away into the **night** with the precious marionette, leaving behind only the dark mask **Holger** clutched **sadly** in his paws.

FRIENDS LIKE BEFORE!

The situation seemed truly hopeless.

"I can't believe it!" cried Paulina in **distress**. "They made off with the *princess*!"

"And my father is still missing!" said Kumi, **SHAKING** her snout. "What can we do?"

The answer came in a soft squeak behind them. "You can ask all the rodents who love you to help you deal with this **CHALLENGE**."

The mouselets and Holger turned around. It was **Sakura**!

After she'd left the THEA SISTERS and Holger **locked** in the Art and Dance Club room, Sakura had begun looking for Kumi. She'd caught sight of her friend leaving the academy grounds and had followed her.

"Kumi, I'm so sorry — I've been really **selfish**!" confessed **Sakura**. "Instead of listening to you, I only thought of myself!" She turned to *Colette*, *Nicky*, PAMELA, PAULINA, and **Violet**. "I was the one who locked you in the club room. Ever since you arrived at the academy, I've been **JEALOUS** of your friendship with **KUMI**, but that's no excuse for the way I treated you."

KUMI forgave her friend immediately. "I was wrong, too, Sakura. I made a **serious** mistake by not telling you the truth! I only wanted to protect you, but I should've trusted you and told you what was really going on."

Full of *emotion*, Sakura hugged her friend tight. Then she turned toward the THEA SISTERS. "Can you mouselings ever forgive me?"

"Of course we can, SISTER!" Pam answered for the group. "We got off on the wrong paw, but that's no reason we can't make up for **lost** time. Let's be friends."

The mouselings all

shook paws, happy to have made a new friend.

In the meantime, **Holger** was preoccupied with the mask he was holding. "But of course! That's who it was!" he exclaimed suddenly, hitting his paw against his snout. "We can still save your father, **KUMI**! I know who **RATNAPPED** him and stole the princess!"

LET'S EVALUATE THE SITUATION

1) Mr. Ishikuro wanted to buy Mr. Nakamura's precious marionette, but Kumi's father refused to give it up.

2) When Mr. Nakamura was ratnapped, Mr. Ishikuro seemed anxious to get the Thea Sisters off the case.

3) It was Mr. Ishikuro's idea to trap the ratnappers. But he never showed up to follow through, and neither did the police!

4) Where have we seen the rat whose mask Holger ripped off?

A PLAN OF ATTACK

"It's all becoming clear!" declared Holger. "The ransom . . . that's why the meeting with the **RATNAPPERS** was set for Kyoto. Mr. Ishikuro lives near here, and he must have known the princess's **HIDING PLACE** was in the area."

He waved the scoundrel's mask. "The proof is in the **cheese pudding**! I knew I'd **seen** that rodent's snout before somewhere, and I just remembered where. One of the **RATNAPPERS** is Mr. Ishikuro's driver!"

"**NO!** I don't believe it!" Kumi was very upset. "I've never liked Mr. Ishikuro, but he's always been a **LOYAL** friend to my father."

"But Holger's theory makes sense!" Paulina interjected. "When we met him, Mr. Ishikuro

THE UNMASKED RATNAPPER IS MR. ISHIKURO'S DRIVER!

was trying to convince your father to **SELL** the *princess*."

"Uh-huh!" Violet agreed. "And after the **RATNAPPING**, he was awfully quick to get us out of Tokyo. In fact, he was a little *too* quick!"

"Not to mention his great plan to intercept

the **RATNAPPERS**," concluded Nicky, folding her paws across her chest. "Where was he when we needed him?"

The **EVIDENCE** all seemed to point to Mr. Ishikuro.

"It's awful!" protested Colette. "Mr. Ishikuro got away with it, and Kumi's father is still **MISSING**!"

"Oh, we're not done with that rat burglar yet!" Pam declared. She was more **DETERMINED** than ever.

The little group returned to the academy to brainstorm a new plan. They gathered in the Art and Dance Club room.

On the walk back, **KUMI** had been thinking about where her father and the *princess* would be kept. "Listen, mouselets, I know Mr. Ishikuro's house well. It's a few hours outside of KYOTO, near Mount Fuji.

That's where he keeps all his **treasures**. If my father and the *princess* aren't there, then I'll be a gerbil's **grandmother!**"

"We must go there **IMMEDIATELY,**" said Violet decisively.

The mouselings said good-bye to Sakura, who agreed to remain at the academy to explain their absence to the professors.

KUMI and the **THEA SISTERS** headed to

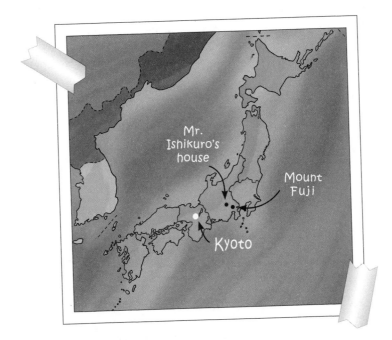

the Kyoto **train station** to meet Holger.

As before, the view of Mount Fuji was breathtaking. The slopes were still covered with a bit of **SNOW**, and the peak was surrounded by low-hanging clouds.

"Let's hope Mount Fuji is sending us some good **LUCK**!" Nicky said.

By the time the mice arrived at their destination, it was dawn. As the sun's glow lit up the mountainside, the seven friends arrived at the home of Mr. Ishikuro. It was a three-story building that resembled a feudal Japanese castle. It was slender and surrounded by tall, rough **STONE** walls decorated with **inlaid** colored wood. The sloped roof tiles reflected the **bright** light of the sun.

"**Moldy Brie** on a baguette, that's some fortress!" commented Colette.

"Getting in there will be no **joke**,"

observed Paulina. "But have no fear, mouselings. I have a **PLAN**!"

Paulina took a sheet of paper out of her pocket and drew a map of the **CASTLE**. "I did a little research on my MousePhone on

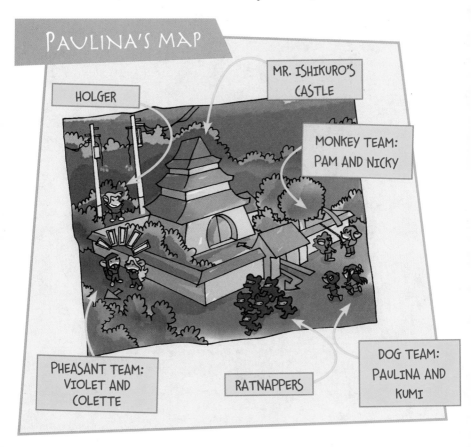

PAULINA'S MAP

HOLGER

MR. ISHIKURO'S CASTLE

MONKEY TEAM: PAM AND NICKY

PHEASANT TEAM: VIOLET AND COLETTE

RATNAPPERS

DOG TEAM: PAULINA AND KUMI

the train ride. The castle has a state-of-the-rat **ALARM** system."

Holger took the map and looked at it carefully. Then, to lighten the mood, he said, "Fortunately, we have some legendary heroes to help us — the *warrior monkey, pheasant, and dog,* just as in the story of Momotaro!"

The seven rodents huddled together to work out a detailed plan of action. Each had a critical task to achieve for the plan to **work**.

The mice got into position.

The moment had arrived to settle the score!

CODE NAME:
MOMOTARO

Holger was the first to swing into action. He snuck to the castle's power box and cut the electricity, disabling the alarm system for a few minutes.

As soon as the castle was completely **DARK**, the guards ran out. The guards

HOLGER CUT THE ELECTRICITY . . .

were the six **RATNAPPERS** who had taken Mr. Nakamura!

At that point, the Pheasant team came on the scene. Violet and Colette scurried over to a wall far from the entrance and got the attention of the **guards** by yelling and making faces at them.

The reaction was immediate. As a group, the six mice scampered toward the two

2

THEN VIOLET AND COLETTE GOT THE GUARDS' ATTENTION . . .

PHEASANT TEAM

mouselings, who quickly **HID** between the trees before the ratnappers could catch up.

Now it was the monkey team's turn!

Nicky and Pam, the most **ATHLETIC** of the group, threw two heavy *ropes* over the **STONE** wall surrounding the castle. During the general confusion, they scaled the wall and leaped **lightly** to the ground. And just in time, too: The guards had activated the

3

WHILE NICKY AND PAM CLIMBED THE STONE WALL TO OPEN THE DOOR FROM THE INSIDE . . .

MONKEY TEAM

SO PAULINA AND KUMI WERE ABLE TO GET IN AND FIND THE CASTLE'S SECURITY CENTER!

DOG TEAM

castle's **EMERGENCY** generator, and the **lights** had come back on.

Pam and Nicky were **easily** able to open the door and let in the dog team: Paulina and Kumi. The last two mouselings had the most **CHALLENGING** task: finding the castle's security center and trapping the **GUARDS** inside their own **DUNGEON**!

"This way!" Paulina hissed. "Let's look behind that door."

Nervously, **KUMI** swung the door open. Before them lay a room filled with **COMPUTERS** and **video monitors**. "This is it!"

BEHIND BARS!

Meanwhile, Violet, Colette, and Holger had managed to sneak onto the grounds. Now the chase was inside the castle **walls**! The three rodents did what they could to keep the guards busy playing hide-and-seek through the **winding** corridors and **OVERSIZE** rooms.

Paulina and Kumi were studying the computerized **ALARM** system. After a few moments, Paulina found a solution. She immediately called Nicky's cell phone. "**Run** to the hallway that leads to the stables, and make sure the **guards** follow you!"

Nicky was the fastest of the group. She sped down a long, **D A R K** hallway, making sure the guards came after her. As they drew closer to Nicky, heavy steel **bars** fell from above.

KERPLINK! KERPLANK! KERPLUNK!

The guards were **TRAPPED** like rats in a cage!

Paulina had been monitoring Nicky's **MOVEMENTS** on the security system's **COMPUTER SCREENS**. As soon as she'd seen that her friend was safe at the

end of the hallway, she'd blocked off the exit.

What a surprise for the six **CRIMINALS** to find themselves behind bars!

KUMI and PAULINA slapped paws. "YEAAAAHHHHH!!!"

But where was Mr. Ishikuro?

OFF WiTH YOUR MASK!

The mouselets and Holger **quickly** regrouped and began to search the castle, which contained treasures from every century and every country.

"Look at all the **artwork**!" exclaimed Violet. "All this beauty deserves to be in a

museum, where other rodents can see it, not buried here in this **cold** castle!"

"This room is dedicated entirely to JAPANESE art," Holger noticed.

The room was filled with amazing **TREASURES** and precious ceramics lined up in a glass case next to two splendid **ancient** kimonos.

Nicky was examining a series of mannequins depicting characters from the

Noh* theater when she JUMPED. "Wait just a minute!" she exclaimed. "*This* isn't a mannequin!"

"**Father!**" cried Kumi. She scurried over to free her father, who was *tied up* and gagged in the middle of all the ancient mannequins.

Mr. Nakamura SQUEEZED his daughter tight. "Oh, little Kumi, you came all the way here to save me!" Then he hugged Holger, too, and saved a deep bow for the THEA SISTERS. "You have really been quite COURAGEOUS mouselings. I don't know how to thank you!"

"We need to *hurry*!" warned Paulina. "The alarm system has called the POLICE, and we still need to find the *princess* before Ishikuro discovers us!"

* One of the classic forms of Japanese theater.

"Too late, you little CHEESE BALLS!" interrupted someone behind them. It was Mr. Ishikuro, and he was holding the case with the *princess*!

That **rat** had hid in his treasure room at the first sign of **danger**, but now he was TRAPPED: Between him and the door were Holger, Mr. Nakamura, and the six young warrior mouselings!

Mr. Nakamura advanced on him threateningly. "How could you do this to me?!" he asked. "I thought you were my **friend**!"

Mr. Ishikuro glanced nervously at the door. But the **MOUSELINGS** and **Holger** stood in his way.

"You don't understand!" he snapped in irritation. "I *had* to have this marionette! It belongs here, with my 𝕥𝕣𝕖𝕒𝕤𝕦𝕣𝕖𝕤!"

Holger shot him a nasty look. "A Bunraku marionette needs to come to life with the eMoTioNS that only true artists with skill and **heart** can share with the public!" he said passionately. "It isn't right to lock her up in a room where no one can **SEE HER**."

Mr. Nakamura looked fondly at his faithful **apprentice**. Understanding and admiration **shone** in his eyes. At last he had realized that his ancient Bunraku tradition would be safer in Holger's paws than in anyone else's.

The Nakamura School had just found a worthy successor!

in PAWCUFFS!

But Mr. Ishikuro had no intention of giving up. He **shot** another sneaky glance toward the door.

"You little mice have **RUINED** everything!" he hissed, scowling at the THEA SISTERS. With those words, he scampered toward the door in an attempt to **ESCAPE**. Colette, Nicky, PAMELA, PAULINA, and **Violet** immediately **leaped** after him, and Violet managed to trip him. As Mr. Ishikuro fell to the floor, the case with the precious marionette slipped from his paws.

For a **LOOOOOONG** instant, they all held their breath as the case FLEW over their heads.

"**NOOOOOOOO!!!!!!**" cried Kumi.

The case opened in midair, and the princess tumbled toward the floor, where she was sure to break into a thousand **PIECES**!

Disaster seemed inevitable, but Pamela *MOVED* fast. Quicker than a cat cornering a mouse, she **POUNCED**, catching the princess right before she hit the ground!

"**YES!**" the mouselings cheered in unison.

Kumi's father tackled Mr. Ishikuro before he could escape.

Holger helped Pam **get up**. Then he carefully cradled the marionette in his paws. "The princess is safe!" he exclaimed.

Colette, Nicky, PAMELA, PAULINA, **Violet**, and **KUMI** sighed in relief.

As for Mr. Ishikuro, he was **ANGRY**. He scowled at the THEA SISTERS. "I almost got away with it!"

"It's a good thing we were able to help stop you," Colette said.

Pam nodded. "There's only one place for slimy sewer rats like you!"

"In **PAWCUFFS**!" the mouselings cried.

At that moment, three police cars with blaring sirens pulled into the courtyard. The

police found the six furious guards already behind bars and a **VERY DISAPPOINTED** Mr. Ishikuro tied up and ready to be taken away!

Over the next few days, the police examined all the *artwork* in the castle. They discovered many stolen treasures that belonged to the JAPANESE people. The castle itself was seized by the authorities and would soon become a **BEAUTIFUL** museum open to lovers of Japanese ART and TRADITION.

THANK YOU, MOUSELINGS!

Now that they had saved her, the THEA SISTERS were finally able to admire the famous *princess* of the Bunraku theater.

"She's *beautiful*!" exclaimed Colette.

The princess's kimono sparkled with a thousand **golden** threads. It was covered with luminous blossoms that looked so real you could almost believe they'd just drifted from a **cherry tree**.

Holger looked at **KUMI**, and she nodded: The moment had arrived to return the princess to her rightful owner.

Holger **CROSSED** the room with a solemn expression. He stopped in front of his teacher and bowed deeply, holding the marionette out to Mr. Nakamura. "It's time for the *princess* to come home, master!"

Mr. Nakamura shook his snout **gently** but firmly. "In your paws, she is *already* home, Holger. The princess is yours now!"

At first, **Holger** couldn't **BELIEVE** his ears. When he understood at last, he began thanking his teacher with a thousand deep **BOWS**.

KUMI was the first to congratulate the

new master of the Nakamura School. "This is a *dream* come true, Holger! No one deserves it more than you do!"

"Speaking of a dream come true, it seems like a *mouseling* we know will soon be leaving for Paris!" whispered Nicky.

Hearing those words, Kumi *timidly* lifted her eyes toward her father. When she saw him *smile*, she raced into his paws. "Thank you, Father! **Thank you so much!**"

Mr. Nakamura shook his snout and patted his daughter's fur. "Don't thank me, thank your **precious** friends! They helped me realize that making you stay here would be like shutting up the princess in a **frozen** prison like Ishikuro's castle!"

Kumi spread her paws wide, as if to hug all five of her friends at once. **"THANK YOU, MOUSELINGS!"**

PARTY TiME!

You can't miss it!

As soon as they got back to Yoshimune Academy, my **dear** mouselings called me to fill me in on their fabumouse **adventure** under the cherry blossoms. They told me so much about Kumi and Sakura that I started to feel as though I already knew them. Then they mentioned the **DANCE** they had been preparing for the annual *yosakoi* festival.

Colette was **SO EXCiTED**. "You absolutely *can't* miss it, Thea!"

"We made a costume just for you, and we have sent it to **NEW MOUSE CiTY** by MousExpress!" added Nicky.

"Yeah!" Paulina said. "Hurry up and buy your plane ticket. Mercury will get you the package just in time for your **departure**!"

"We're waiting for you, Thea!" they yelled as they hung up.

So now you understand what was in the package that came from Japan! It was a **splendid** traditional costume *Colette*, *nicky*, PAMELA, PAULINA, **Violet**, and their **friends** had created for me to wear to the *yosakoi* festival!

When I arrived, the town of Kochi was bright with a thousand COLORS. The music of each group filled the air with *happiness*.

Kumi and Sakura took me in as an honored guest and helped me learn their choreography. Even **Holger**

danced with us, while Mr. Nakamura followed us from afar, **PROUD** of his daughter's talent.

So many rodents, **COLORS**, and dances!

It was really a special event for all of us. JAPAN would always have a place in our **hearts**!

They were more than friends. They were sisters!

Thea Sisters

Want to read the next adventure
of the Thea Sisters?
I can't wait to tell you all about it!

THEA STILTON AND THE
STAR CASTAWAYS

A professor at Mouseford Academy is
organizing a trip to outer space, and the
Thea Sisters are invited. The mouselings are
headed on a fabumouse mission...to the
moon! After much preparation, the mice
blast off. But when they arrive at their lunar
vacation spot, things start to go wrong,
including spaceship wrecks and rebellious
robots. Can the Thea Sisters save the day?

And don't miss any of my other fabumouse adventures!

THEA STILTON AND THE DRAGON'S CODE

THEA STILTON AND THE MOUNTAIN OF FIRE

THEA STILTON AND THE GHOST OF THE SHIPWRECK

THEA STILTON AND THE SECRET CITY

THEA STILTON AND THE MYSTERY IN PARIS

Want to read my next adventure?
I can't wait to tell you all about it!

SAVE THE WHITE WHALE!

Holey cheese, did I need a vacation! I had been working my tail off at *The Rodent's Gazette,* and I really needed a break. So I invited Petunia Pretty Paws to visit the Bay of Whales with me. But our trip got off on the wrong paw, and my relaxing vacation turned into a real nightmare. That is, until Petunia and I came across a great white whale that needed our help. This would be one adventure I'd never forget!

And don't miss any of my other fabumouse adventures!

#1 LOST TREASURE OF THE EMERALD EYE

#2 THE CURSE OF THE CHEESE PYRAMID

#3 CAT AND MOUSE IN A HAUNTED HOUSE

#4 I'M TOO FOND OF MY FUR!

#5 FOUR MICE DEEP IN THE JUNGLE

#6 PAWS OFF, CHEDDARFACE!

#7 RED PIZZAS FOR A BLUE COUNT

#8 ATTACK OF THE BANDIT CATS

#9 A FABUMOUSE VACATION FOR GERONIMO

#10 ALL BECAUSE OF A CUP OF COFFEE

#11 IT'S HALLOWEEN, YOU 'FRAIDY MOUSE!

#12 MERRY CHRISTMAS, GERONIMO!

#13 THE PHANTOM OF THE SUBWAY

#14 THE TEMPLE OF THE RUBY OF FIRE

#15 THE MONA MOUSA CODE

#16 A CHEESE-COLORED CAMPER

#17 WATCH YOUR WHISKERS, STILTON!

#18 SHIPWRECK ON THE PIRATE ISLANDS

#19 MY NAME IS STILTON, GERONIMO STILTON

#20 SURF'S UP, GERONIMO!

#21 THE WILD, WILD WEST

#22 THE SECRET OF CACKLEFUR CASTLE

A CHRISTMAS TALE

#23 VALENTINE'S DAY DISASTER

#24 FIELD TRIP TO NIAGARA FALLS

#25 THE SEARCH FOR SUNKEN TREASURE

#26 THE MUMMY WITH NO NAME

#27 THE CHRISTMAS TOY FACTORY

#28 WEDDING CRASHER

#29 DOWN AND OUT DOWN UNDER

#30 THE MOUSE ISLAND MARATHON

#31 THE MYSTERIOUS CHEESE THIEF

CHRISTMAS CATASTROPHE

#32 VALLEY OF THE GIANT SKELETONS

#33 GERONIMO AND THE GOLD MEDAL MYSTERY

#34 GERONIMO STILTON, SECRET AGENT

#35 A VERY MERRY CHRISTMAS

#36 GERONIMO'S VALENTINE

#37 THE RACE ACROSS AMERICA

#38 A FABUMOUSE SCHOOL ADVENTURE

#39 SINGING SENSATION

#40 THE KARATE MOUSE

#41 MIGHTY MOUNT KILIMANJARO

#42 THE PECULIAR PUMPKIN THIEF

#43 I'M NOT A SUPERMOUSE!

#44 THE GIANT DIAMOND ROBBERY

Coming soon!

#45 SAVE THE WHITE WHALE!

Don't miss
these very
special editions!

THE
KINGDOM
OF FANTASY

THE
QUEST FOR
PARADISE:
THE RETURN TO
THE KINGDOM OF
FANTASY

THANKS FOR READING,
AND GOOD-BYE UNTIL OUR
NEXT ADVENTURE!

THEA SISTERS